23 24 25 26
22
21
20
19
18
17
16
15
4

Edward 1
Edward 2
Edward 3
Thomas 1
Thomas 2
Thomas 3

Take turns to roll the dice. If you roll a 2, move
a truck 2 spaces along the track.
If you roll a 5, move 5 spaces.

When you get a truck to the end of the track,
put it in the Yard, then go back
for another one.
The winner is the first player to get 3 trucks
into their part of the Yard.

£6.99
UK only

A message from Thomas

"Peep, peep!"

"Hello, and welcome to my super new annual. There are lots of stories with my engine friends, like Edward, Henry, Gordon, James – and little Percy, of course!

There are stories about Duncan, Elizabeth the Lorry, and Cranky the Crane, too – and I mustn't forget Bertie the Bus!

Inside, you'll also find lots of puzzle pages, and games as well. I think they are lots of fun, and I hope you do, too!"

THOMAS & FRIENDS

Annual 2004

This book belongs to

Luke Thomas Agar

My favourite engine is

Thomas

I also like

Percy , Gordon

and

James , Henry

Contents

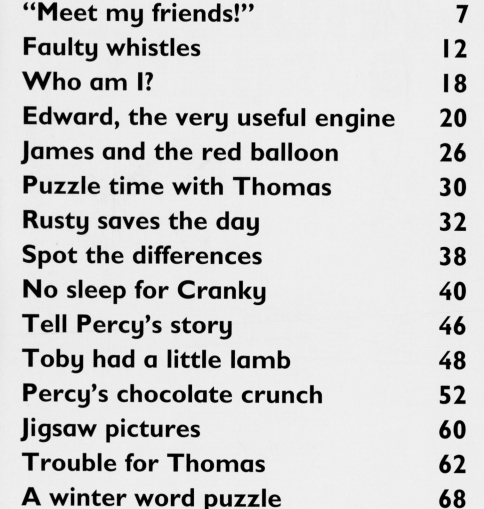

Don't forget to enter the Thomas and Friends Annual competition. There are super prizes to be won. You'll find it at the back of the book.

Written by Brenda Apsley
Edited by Brenda Apsley and Jane Clempner
Designed by Helen Prole

Thomas the Tank Engine & Friends

A BRITT ALLCROFT COMPANY PRODUCTION

Based on The Railway Series by The Rev W Awdry

© Gullane (Thomas) LLC 2003

Photographs © Gullane (Thomas) Limited 2003

Published in Great Britain 2003 by Egmont Books Limited, 239 Kensington High Street, London W8 6SA

Printed in Dubai, the U.A.E.
ISBN 0 7498 5845 1
10 9 8 7 6 5 4 3 2 1

"Meet my friends!"

This is Sir Topham Hatt, but we call him **The Fat Controller**. He's in charge of the railway.

2

Edward is the old Number 2 engine. He's very kind.

Number 3 is **Henry**. He's very fast!

This is **Gordon**, Number 4,
who pulls the Express Train.

This Really Splendid Engine
is **James**, the red Number 5.

Happy **Percy**, Number 6,
is my special engine friend.

Toby is a Tram Engine.
His coach is called Henrietta.

Duncan
is a little tank engine, just like me!

Number 8's real name is Montague –
but we all call him **Duck**!

Do you know who this is?
Yes, it's **Peter Sam**!

This is **Rheneas**. As usual, he's with
his special friend, **Skarloey**.

This is **Elizabeth** the Lorry. She works at the Quarry.

Rusty the diesel works at the Quarry, too.

Stepney was saved from the scrap yard by Rusty.

Bertie the bright red bus is a special friend of mine.

So is good old **Terence**, the tractor.

Cranky the crane works at the docks.

So does **Salty** the diesel. He just loves telling stories!

Bill and **Ben** are twins who work on the line between the clay pits and the harbour.

Harvey is a crane engine. He's very useful.

This is **Harold** the helicopter. I call him Whirlybird, because he can fly!

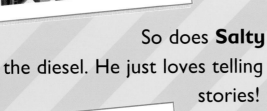
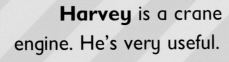

Faulty whistles

It was a very early morning on Sodor, and the sun was just beginning to light up the sky.

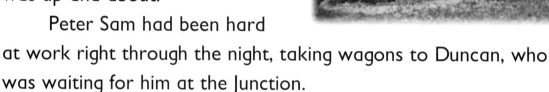

Most people were still asleep, but one of the engines was up and about.

Peter Sam had been hard at work right through the night, taking wagons to Duncan, who was waiting for him at the Junction.

Duncan was building up steam while he waited for Peter Sam to bring the rest of his load. He had an important job to do. He was going to take the wagons, as usual, but today he had another passenger. He was taking the new organ to Strawberry Grove School. The Headmaster, Mr Hastings, was going with him, to make sure that it got there safely.

Peter Sam was nearly at the Junction when he went under a low tree branch at the side of the track. Bump! The branch knocked Peter Sam's whistle off!

"Bother!" said Peter Sam. "I can't run on the tracks without my whistle. It wouldn't be safe."

Duncan agreed with him. "That's right," he said. "An engine has to have his whistle. It's the whistle that makes the engine." And just to prove it, he let off a big blast on his own whistle. He was very proud of it. "PEEP!"

Peter Sam and the other engines didn't take any notice. They didn't think Duncan was very helpful, so they ignored him.

"Hmph!" said Duncan, and as soon as his wagons were loaded, off he puffed. He was in a bit of a huff.

Duncan steamed along by the fields and woods. He was still in a bit of a huff. "The others are just jealous of my whistle," he said. "They know it's the best one of all." And just to prove it, he whistled at some sheep. "PEEP!"

But the sheep didn't take any notice of him. They were too busy eating grass.

"Bah!" said Duncan. "Silly sheep! I'll whistle much louder next time."

Elizabeth the Lorry was waiting at the level crossing with a big bull in her box.

When Duncan saw them, he whistled as loudly as he could. "PEEEEEEP!"

"Moooooooo!" said the bull.

"Stop making that noise, Duncan!" said Elizabeth.

Duncan didn't say anything.

"I don't care if Elizabeth and the others don't like my whistle," said Duncan. "It's going to be the loudest on the whole island."

Duncan was so pleased with himself that he didn't notice that his whistle was coming loose. It wobbled around from side to side.

When he went round a corner and saw Terence the Tractor working in the field, he was very pleased. "He'll get my loudest and longest whistle yet!" he said.

Duncan blew as hard as he could ... and his wobbly whistle shot off into the air, like a little rocket!

Duncan stopped. "It's my whistle," he told his Driver. "I blew it, and it flew up into the air!"

Duncan's Driver and Fireman looked for the whistle. So did Terence's Driver, and so did Headmaster Hastings. They looked everywhere, but the whistle was nowhere to be seen.

"We're stuck now!" said Duncan's Driver. "We can't move along the track without a whistle. It's not safe."

No one knew quite what to do, until Headmaster Hastings had an idea. "Leave it to me," he said. "I know how we can let people know that we're coming."

Can you guess what he did?

Yes, every time Duncan needed to whistle, Headmaster Hastings played a note on the big school organ.

Duncan didn't make another sound for the rest of the day, but Headmaster Hastings did!

When Duncan came to a crossing, Headmaster Hastings tooted on the organ. TOOT!

When Duncan stopped at a station, Headmaster Hastings tooted on the organ. TOOT!

When Duncan came into the sidings, Headmaster Hastings tooted to warn people. TOOT!

The organ worked just as well as a whistle – though Duncan didn't think so, of course!

Duncan did all his deliveries, but he was much quieter than usual. He didn't like having an organ toot instead of a whistle.

When he steamed back to the Junction, Rusty, Rheneas, Skarloey and Peter Sam were waiting for him.

Poor Duncan felt silly when Headmaster Hastings played the organ again. TOOOOOOT!

Rusty laughed. "Look," he said, "it's Duncan, the Musical Engine!"

"Let's whistle along with him," said Rheneas.

"Yes, let's," said Skarloey. "TOOT, TOOT. Come on, Peter Sam, you can join in."

Peter Sam had a shiny new whistle by now, but he didn't blow it. He felt sorry for Duncan.

"You did really well to do all your work without a whistle, Duncan," he said.

That made Duncan feel a little bit more cheerful. "Do you really think so, Peter Sam?" he asked.

"Yes I do!" said Peter Sam. "You know, it's not the whistle that makes the engine – it's the engine that makes the whistle!"

"Or the organ!" said Headmaster Hastings, and he played an extra loud TOOOOOOOT!

That made all the engines laugh and laugh – even Duncan!

Who am I?

Who do these clues tell you about?
Say or write the names, and point to
the ones you can see in the picture.

1

I am blue.
I am a tank engine.
I have a number 1
on my side.
Who am I?

_____

2

I am red.
I have 4 wheels.
I am a bus.
Who am I?

_____

3

I am a red engine.
I have the number 5
on my side.
I'm a really Splendid Engine.
Who am I?

_____

4

I am green.
I am engine number 6.
I like working with the
trucks in the Yard.
Who am I?

_____

5

I work at
the Quarry.
I am an orange diesel engine.
My name begins with R.
Who am I?

_____

ANSWERS:

1. Thomas 2. Bertie 3. James 4. Percy 5. Rusty

Edward, the very useful engine

1 Thomas and his friends are good at different things. Gordon is strong and fast, so he pulls the big Express Train. Little Percy is good at carrying the mail.

Edward works with the trucks. He's a good Back Engine, too. When the engines have heavy loads to pull, he helps them. He couples up behind, at the back, and pushes.

2 But Edward is old, and some of the engines think he can't work as hard as he used to.

"He's a useless old steam pot!" said Gordon. "He should be retired."

"Re-tyred?" said Percy. "But he doesn't have tyres!"

"No, RETIRED," said Thomas. "It means taken out of service, not used any more."

3 Later on, Percy told his Driver what Gordon had said about Edward. "The big engines don't think he's useful anymore. They say he should be retired."

When Percy's Driver told The Fat Controller what Gordon had said, he was not at all pleased.

"Edward, retired?" he said. "I will see about that!"

4 The Fat Controller went to speak to Edward. "The new Loop Line is finished now, Edward," he said. "I want you to teach Stepney how to run it properly."

"But who will look after the trucks, Sir?" Edward asked.

"Duck will do your work for you," said The Fat Controller.

5 When the big engines heard the news, they were pleased.
"It's good that Duck is taking Edward's place," said Henry. "Duck is very reliable."

"Yes," said Gordon. "But it makes no difference to me, because I don't go near the trucks. And I never need a Back Engine. WHEEESH!"

6 Edward was happy with his new job. He liked working on the Loop Line with Stepney.

It was good fun taking lots of passengers out into the countryside. He enjoyed stopping at all the little stations to let people get on and off.

7 But Duck was not so happy. He was pulling the trucks up a steep hill on Gordon's line, and they were making fun of him. They sang:

"Duck should play with other ducks,

'Cos he's no good at pulling trucks!

Quack, quack, hold back!"

8 It was very hard work pulling the trucks. Duck went slower ... and slower ... and slower. Halfway up the hill, his wheels stopped turning altogether!

"Oh, no," said his Driver. "We're stuck, and this is Gordon's line. He'll be coming along this way any minute now!"

He phoned the Signalman to warn him that Duck was stuck.

9 But it was too late to switch Gordon to the other line. "I'll just have to put all the signals to red," said the Signalman. "That will stop him."

10 Gordon saw the red signals. He had to stop, but he didn't want to. "This hill is steep," he said. "If I stop, I'll never get started again."

He was right. When he tried to set off again, his wheels spun and spun.

"We need some help," said his Driver. "We need a Back Engine."

"Bah!" said Gordon.

11 The Fat Controller sent Edward to help. He buffered up to Gordon and Duck, and pushed them all the way back to the Station.

A little boy pointed at Edward. "That Back Engine must be the strongest of them all," he said.

The Fat Controller told Gordon off. "You said rude things about Edward," he said. "But he has proved that he is reliable, and VERY useful."

12 Gordon had to agree. He rolled up to Edward and said, "Thank you for helping me. You really are a very useful engine."

"It was nothing," said Edward. "I was glad to help."

Soon, things were back to normal. Edward was back at his old job. And there was no more talk of him being old and ready for retiring ...

James and the red balloon

You can read this story yourself. There are little pictures in place of some of the words, to help you.

One day,  **1** went to bring something

from the docks. "Toot!" said  **2** .

"What have you got there?"

"It's a  **3** ," said Thomas. "A big one,

filled with hot air. It has a  **4** under it

that **5** can ride in."

ANSWERS: 1. Thomas 2. Percy 3. balloon 4. basket 5. people

26

The balloon floated up into the 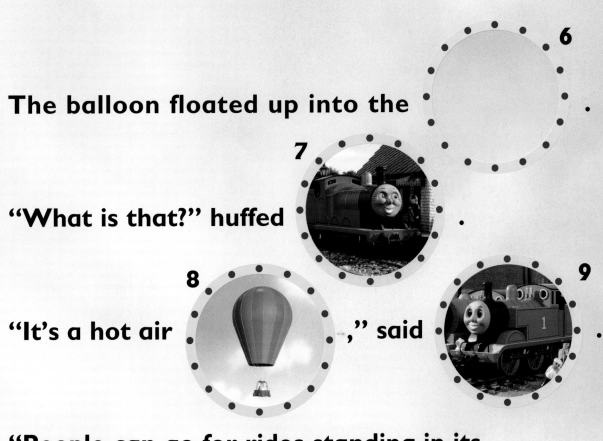 .

"What is that?" huffed .

"It's a hot air ," said .

"People can go for rides standing in its

." The big red balloon

floated up into the and over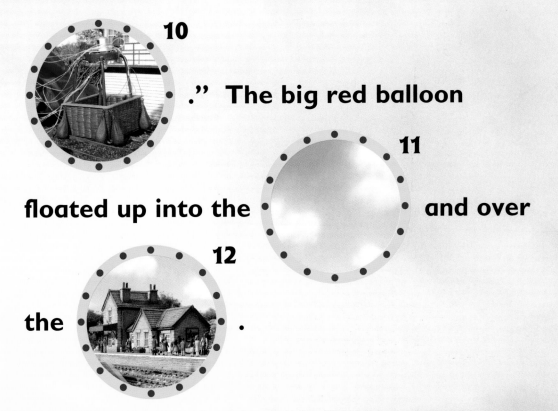

the .

Then it went over the  **13** . Lots of

14

watched it. "OOOH!" they said.

15

"Look!" watched for so long

16

that he nearly ran into !

17

was talking to Thomas

18

when all of a sudden the fell down

19

from the . It had no hot air left!

The balloon landed on 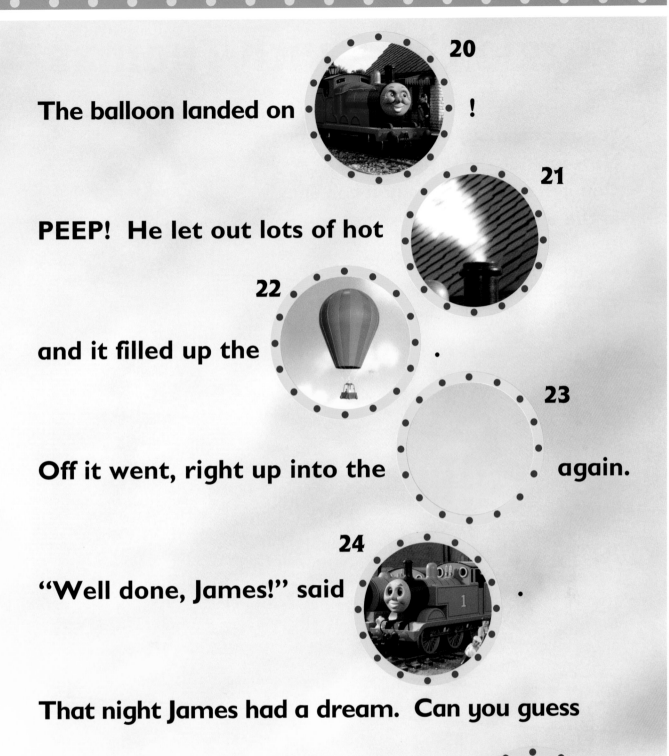 !

PEEP! He let out lots of hot

and it filled up the .

22

Off it went, right up into the **23** again.

24

"Well done, James!" said .

That night James had a dream. Can you guess

what it was about? Yes, the big red **25** !

Puzzle time with Thomas

"Look at the big picture on this page.
Now look at the little pictures.
Can you tick the ones you can see
in the big picture?"

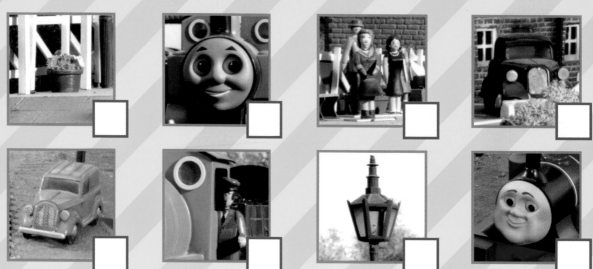

"Now look at the big picture on this page,
then at the little pictures. Can you tick five
little things that are in the big picture?"

Rusty saves the day

Rusty is a little diesel engine who works at the Quarry. His best friends are called Rheneas and Skarloey.

Rusty loves helping them keep their little line clear. But sometimes he's so busy helping them that he forgets all about his own work at the Quarry.

One day when Rusty got back from helping Rheneas and Skarloey, The Fat Controller was waiting for him.

"Where have you been?" asked The Fat Controller. "You should be working here, at the Quarry."

"Sorry, Sir," said Rusty. "I was helping clear the line for Rheneas and Skarloey."

"Were you indeed?" said The Fat Controller. "Hmph! That

line is in very bad
condition. I am going
to shut it down."

"But what about
Rheneas and
Skarloey?" asked
Rusty. "What will
happen to them?"

"They can come
and work at the
Quarry with you," said The Fat Controller.

Rheneas and Skarloey were sorry that their line was closed.
They were not happy working at the Quarry. They missed the
forests and hills near their line. But most of all they missed the
passengers.

Rusty felt very sorry for them.

The next time The Fat Controller went to the Quarry, he had some important news.

"There will be rock blasting here for the next two weeks," he told the engines. "It will not be safe for you here, so I will find other work for you to do."

Rusty thought about the kind of work he would like to do. "Please, Sir," he said. "Can we repair Rheneas and Skarloey's line? I know they would like to go back to their old jobs."

The Fat Controller thought about Rusty's idea.

"All right, you can do it," he said. Then he looked at Rusty. "But you must do the work in two weeks," he said. "Then you must come back to work at the Quarry."

"Yes, I will," said Rusty. "Thank you, Sir."

Rusty and the others worked very hard. They cleared rocks and branches from Rheneas and Skarloey's line. Then they mended breaks in the track.

All the jobs took a long time.

One day Elizabeth the Lorry drove past on her way to the tip. "What a waste of time," she said. "You'll never get this line back in good working order."

Skarloey looked at the rocks and branches that were still on the line. "Elizabeth is right," he said sadly.

Rheneas looked at the bits of track that were still broken. "Yes, she's right," he said. "We'll never get the work done in time."

"But we can't give up!" said Rusty. "We'll just have to work harder than ever."

When Rusty saw Elizabeth again the next day, he had an idea. "What we need is a lorry to help us," he said.

Elizabeth stopped. "But I can't help you," she said. "I'm a Quarry lorry."

"Yes, what we need is a very SPECIAL kind of lorry," said Rusty.

"But I'M a very special kind of lorry," said Elizabeth. "Look at my big tipper box!"

Rusty looked doubtful. "But we need a lorry who can haul things," he said.

"I can haul things!" said Elizabeth.

"And we need a lorry who can pull heavy branches," said Rusty.

"I can pull heavy branches," said Elizabeth. "VERY heavy branches."

Rusty smiled. "So you'll do it?" he said. "You'll help us?"

"Of course I will!" said Elizabeth.

Elizabeth worked very hard helping Rusty and his friends. She hauled away rocks and rubbish.

She pulled branches off the line.

She even moved a big tree that had fallen across the track.

It took the rest of the two weeks, but the line was soon as good as new.

"Thank you, Elizabeth," said Rusty. "We couldn't have done it without you!"

Elizabeth was very pleased. "I know!" she said.

When The Fat Controller came to look at the line, he was very pleased, too. "Well done, all of you," he said. "We will open the line again right away."

Rusty felt very proud. So did Elizabeth.

Rheneas and Skarloey were proud, too. They were very happy to be going back to work on their own line again.

"I suppose I'll have to come and keep the line clear for you," said Elizabeth. But she didn't mind really, because she had enjoyed herself.

"And there is someone else who is going back to his old job," said The Fat Controller. "Yes, off you go, Rusty, back to the Quarry!"

Spot the differences

1

The pictures on these pages look the same, but there are 8 things that are different in picture 2.

2

Look carefully –
can you find them all?

No sleep for Cranky

The docks on the island of Sodor are always very busy. Ships and boats come and go with animals and passengers and all kinds of goods. There are jobs to be done every day of the year.

Cranky the crane works at the docks. He works through the day, then he works through the night as well. He never gets a good rest. He never has the time to take a nap, so he's always tired. He works and works and works.

Cranky has very tall legs. He's up high and all the engines are down below, so he doesn't have any real friends. The only things he sees are the seagulls that fly around him and sometimes sit on his arms.

Cranky doesn't have much fun. He doesn't have much to smile about. And that's why he's always cranky.

When Salty, the dockyard diesel, arrived one day, Cranky was hard at work, as usual. He was unloading big pipes on to some trucks.

"Ahoy there, Cranky!" said Salty.

Cranky didn't say hello. "You're late!" he snapped. "Where have you been?"

"Oh, dear," said Salty. "Cranky old Cranky."

When Bill and Ben arrived, Cranky didn't say hello to them, either. "Hurry up!" he said. "I haven't got all day!"

"You're no fun," said Bill.

"You wouldn't be fun if you were stuck up here, like me!" said Cranky.

"I think you're lonely," said Ben.

"Yes," said Salty. "Now that reminds me of one of my favourite stories."

"Oh, no, not another one of your stories!" said Cranky – but Salty told it anyway.

"It was a wee naughty storm," said Salty. "The likes of which you only see once ..."

Salty's story went on ... and on ... and on ...

Listening to it made Cranky even more cranky than usual.

He got so angry that he swung his arm around and dropped the pipes on to the tracks. They rolled down the track, bumped into the shed with a loud crash – and knocked it down!

Bill, Ben and Salty were trapped!

"Whoops!" said Cranky, looking very pleased with himself.

"You've blown it now, Matey!" said Salty.

"You're going to be in trouble," said Bill.

"Yes, BIG trouble!" said Ben.

Soon after, Thomas arrived with The Fat Controller.

"Just look at this mess!" said The Fat Controller. "We can't move the bits of the shed until the morning. Bill, Ben and Salty will just have to stay here for the night."

"Not to worry," said Salty. "I know a good way of passing the time. Now, did I tell you the wee story about ..."

Cranky groaned. "Oh, no ..."

Night fell, and the sky grew dark, but that didn't stop Salty. He was still telling his story when the moon came out. On and on it went ... on and on and on.

"He sailed round the Cape without a scratch, but then when he got back home, he crashed right in front of my buffers!" said Salty. "Luckily, nothing was damaged ..."

"Nothing except my poor ears!" said Cranky.

If this is what having friends is like, he thought, I don't want any!

When dawn came and the sun appeared in the sky, Salty was STILL telling his story. It went on ... and on ... and on ... and on.

"And then, you just will not believe what happened next ..." he said.

"Please, no more!" said Cranky. "My ears are hurting!"

When Harvey, the crane engine, arrived, Cranky was almost pleased to see him. The Fat Controller had sent him to clear up the mess.

"Flatten my funnel!" said Harvey. "Who dropped all these pipes and stuff?"

"It was Cranky!" said Bill.

"Yes, Cranky!" said Ben.

Cranky watched as Harvey cleared up the mess. He was so pleased that Salty and Bill and Ben would be going soon that he forgot to be cranky.

"I won't misbehave again, I promise," he said. "As long as I don't have to listen to any more of Salty's stories!"

Cranky worked hard for the rest of the day to make up for being naughty. He loaded the trucks carefully and quickly, so that Thomas and the other engines could set off on time. He even said 'please' and 'thank you', which was very unusual!

"Peep!" said Thomas. "This is new! This isn't like Cranky at all!"

But, oh dear, Thomas spoke too soon!

Cranky just couldn't help himself. He dropped the next load on the rails, right in front of Percy!

"Oh well, it was nice while it lasted," said Percy, and all the other engines laughed.

Cranky was just as cranky as ever!

Or was he just pretending?

Tell Percy's story

1 One cold day in winter, Percy goes to get some coal.

2 The tracks are frozen. He can't get back to the Shed.

3 Percy has to stay in the sidings.

4 In the night, snow falls ...

5 What happens to Percy? Look at
the pictures, and tell his story in
your own words.

Toby had a little lamb

It was winter time, and the ground was

covered in .

"This isn't much fun," said

to his coach, .

All of a sudden Toby had to stop. Farmer

McColl was standing at the side of the track.

He was waving a red .

"The roads are blocked with  ,"

said Farmer McColl.

"My  and  are stuck

up on the hill. They need help. Can you

bring a vet,  ?"

"We'll go to the next  and call for help,"

said Toby's . "Off we go, Toby!"

The vet and  **11** were waiting at the

12 . "We have to help the **13** ,"

said Toby. "We will," said the **14** .

"I'll send Duck," said The Fat Controller.

"He has a **15** to help him."

But **16** could not get through

the thick white **17** . He had to turn back!

"I'll go on my old line," said  . "Very well,"

said . The bridge shook, but Toby kept

going. When  saw him he said,

"What a brave engine you are!" The

said, "The and her little

need somewhere warm to rest."

"Put them in my coach,  !" said Toby.

Percy's chocolate crunch

1 The Fat Controller's engines all like to look as neat and clean and tidy as they can – especially James and Thomas. Percy likes to look neat and clean, too, but it's hard for him, because he often has the dirtiest jobs to do.

2 One day The Fat Controller came to talk to the engines. "We must save water," he told them. "No engine can have more than one wash-down a day."

"One a day?" said Percy.

"Yes," said The Fat Controller. "Remember, usefulness comes before cleanliness."

3 Percy wasn't pleased about the news. "But I NEED my wash-downs," he said. "I get dirtier than the others because I have all the messiest jobs."

James made fun of him. "You're a pouty puffer, Percy!" he said.

"No, I'm not!" said Percy, and he chuffed away in a bit of a huff.

4 Percy had to take the trucks to collect some coal. Coal is dirty, messy black stuff, so Percy tried extra hard to stay clean.

But the troublesome trucks played a trick on him. The last truck stopped under the chute where the coal came out. It just would not move.

5 Percy pushed hard, and the trucks moved forward – but Percy ended up under the coal chute!

The coal came down, and Percy was covered in messy black dust that made him cough and splutter.

"Oh, no!" said Percy. "Just look at me! I'm filthy! And I can't have a wash-down until later. I'll just have to carry on like this."

6 As Percy chuffed to the docks, the naughty trucks teased him. "Clackety clack, don't look back, dirty Percy's on our track!" they sang.

Harold the helicopter was taking off as Percy arrived. His long arms whirred and spun around, and they blew a pile of dirty ash that was at the side of the track up into the air.

7   Can you guess where the messy black ash landed? Yes – on poor Percy!

"Oh, no!" said Percy. "Not again. Now I'm even dirtier than I was before! Driver, I want a wash-down! I need one."

"Sorry," said Percy's Driver. "You know what The Fat Controller said. Usefulness comes before cleanliness. You'll just have to wait."

8   Percy's next job was to take a load of sugar to the Sodor Chocolate Factory. He was pleased about that. "At least sugar is nice and clean," he said.

Soon Percy was on his way with the boxcars full of sugar. He went as fast as he could so the wind would blow away some of the messy coal dust and ash.

9 But Percy and his Driver didn't know that a leaky truck had spilled some slippery oil on the track!

Percy sped up to the Chocolate Factory, and his Driver put on the brakes. But Percy couldn't stop! His wheels skidded and spun on the oily rails.

"Oh, no!" hooted Percy, as the buffers got nearer and nearer. "Heeeeeelp! Oh-oooooooo!"

10 Poor Percy! He smashed through the buffers ...

Then he bashed into the factory wall with a big CRASH.

Then he disappeared inside ...

11 There was a loud noise as Percy crashed into something inside the factory. BANG!

Then there was the sound of breaking wood as he steamed right through the doors at the other side of the factory!

12 Poor Percy! He had crashed into a big vat of melted chocolate inside the factory, and now it was all over him. He was covered from funnel to cab in sticky, gooey brown chocolate!

"Oh, yuuuuk!" said Percy. "What a mess! I've never been this dirty and messy before!"

13 Duck pushed Percy on to a turntable on a truck, and took him back to the Sheds.

The other engines couldn't believe their eyes when they saw Percy, and they all laughed.

"You look like a choc-ice on wheels!" said Henry.

"Disgraceful!" said Gordon.

14 The engines all thought seeing a chocolate-covered Percy was very funny – all except Percy, of course.

"Bon-bon Percy!" said James.

Even Percy's friend Thomas couldn't help making fun of him.

"PEEP! You look good enough to eat, Percy!" he hooted.

15 Just then Percy heard another voice: "AHEM!" It was The Fat Controller!

"I see that you have had a bad day, Percy," he said.

"Yes, I have, Sir," replied Percy.

"But you didn't give up," said The Fat Controller. "You kept going. You showed us all that usefulness DOES come before cleanliness."

16 The Fat Controller smiled. "I am very pleased with you, Percy," he said. "Now, you can have your wash-down – AND a brand new coat of paint!"

Percy was so pleased that he couldn't speak. He just beamed a big, big smile.

"Oh!" he said. "OH! OH!"

Jigsaw pictures

"Can you help me complete these jigsaw puzzle pictures? Which pieces will complete each picture?"

1

2

3

4

5

6

ANSWERS: Page 60: Pieces 1 and 5   Page 61: Pieces 3 and 4

Trouble for Thomas

It was winter holiday time, and very cold and snowy, but the engines didn't mind. They loved this time of year, when the railway was decorated with coloured flags and lights, and there were lots and lots of passengers and presents to deliver.

The engines were in the Big Station when Percy puffed in.

"Driver says there's more snow on the way," said Edward.

"Yes, we'll soon be wearing our snow ploughs," said James.

Henry knew that Thomas didn't like his snow plough. "You'll enjoy that, won't you, Thomas?" he asked.

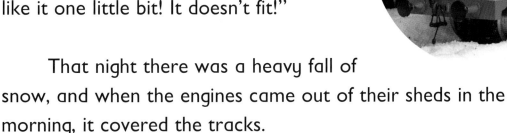

"Peep!" said Thomas, chuffing out of the station. "You know I won't! I don't like it one little bit! It doesn't fit!"

That night there was a heavy fall of snow, and when the engines came out of their sheds in the morning, it covered the tracks.

The Fat Controller told the engines that they would have snow ploughs fitted to help them get through the snow.

He had some other news for Thomas. "I want you to collect something special from the docks," he said. "It's for the village feast on Toby's branch line."

Thomas was pleased about his special job. But he wasn't pleased about his snow plough.

"My snow plough is too big for me, Sir," said Thomas. "Can I please have one that is the right size?"

The Fat Controller shook his head. "There are no spare snow ploughs," he said. "I'm afraid you'll just have to make do, Thomas."

The fitters tried to fit Thomas' snow plough. His Driver and Fireman helped, too. But it was just too big for him, and very uncomfortable.

"Big, horrid old thing!" grumbled Thomas.

Thomas' Driver and the fitters pushed the snow plough in place – and it fell off!

Driver laughed. "We'll just have to try again!" he said.

He was cheerful, but Thomas wasn't. He was grumpy and he pulled a face to show how fed up he was. He didn't like that snow plough one little bit!

Thomas was pleased when he saw what was waiting for him at the docks. It was the biggest Christmas tree he had ever seen!

"It's going to stand right in the middle of the village," Salty told him. "It will have lights and decorations. You make sure you get it to Toby safely, young Thomas!"

Thomas was as excited as Salty. "I will!" he said as he steamed off.

When Thomas arrived at the station with the big tree, Toby was very pleased to see him. "The people in the village will be so pleased when we deliver the tree," he said. "And I'm glad you have your snow plough, Thomas," he added. "I can't clear these deep snow drifts by myself."

Thomas and Toby set off together. It was hard work, pushing through the snow, because Thomas' snow plough wasn't working very well. But they didn't give up, and when they got to the water tower they could see the village in the distance.

But then Thomas got stuck in an extra-deep snow drift.

He pushed the snow aside, harder, harder – but his snow plough started to crack!

The metal creaked ... and bent ... then the bolts that held it on snapped ... and the snow plough swung to the side like a big knife!

The snow plough cut into the water tower, and with a loud crash and a cloud of snow, down it fell!

"Cinders and ashes!" said Thomas. "That wasn't my fault, was it?"

"Of course not," said his Driver. "It was an accident."

Thomas' Driver and Fireman took off what was left of Thomas' snow plough and put it at the side of the track.

"We're well and truly stuck now," said Driver.

"But we must deliver the tree," said Thomas. "Let me try again, without the snow plough. I'm sure I can make it through the snow."

It was very hard for Thomas to force his way through the snow. But he wouldn't give up.

He pushed and pushed.

Then he pushed a little harder.

Then he pushed a little harder still, until ...

Thomas and Toby steamed into the village station!

Everyone was waiting for them, and they clapped and waved.

"Phew!" said Thomas, and he let off an extra loud whistle. "Peep, PEEP!"

The villagers all cheered: "Hooray for Thomas! Hooray for Toby! HOORAY!"

The next day, The Fat Controller sent for Thomas. He was a little worried. What would The Fat Controller say about his broken snow plough?

But Sir Topham wasn't cross at all. No, he was very pleased with Thomas. "The villagers had a wonderful feast," he told him. "And it wouldn't have been the same without the tree. You were very brave to get through all that snow without a snow plough."

Thomas felt very proud. "Thank you, Sir," he said.

"As you know," said The Fat Controller, "there are no spare snow ploughs, so you'll just have to ... do without one!"

Thomas was very pleased. That was the best news of all! "Oh, thank you, Sir!" he said. "PEEP!"

A winter word puzzle

These words are from the Trouble for Thomas story. Can you find them in the word square? They are spelled out from top to bottom, and from side to side.

A	G	T	J	S	F
T	H	O	M	A	S
R	N	B	D	L	N
E	B	Y	L	T	O
E	C	P	S	Y	W
O	M	C	O	L	D

TREE   **SNOW**   **COLD**

THOMAS   **TOBY**   **SALTY**

"Peep!"

"I hope you liked the stories and puzzles in my annual! Goodbye, and see you next year!"

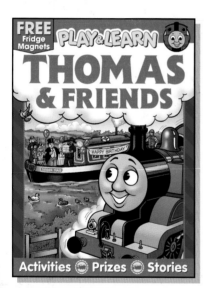